D0254862

NINJA KID 2

FLYING NINJA!

SCHOLASTIC

If you purchased this book without a cover, you should be aware that this book is stolen property. It was reported as "unsold and destroyed" to the publisher, and neither the author nor the publisher has received any payment for this "stripped book."

Text copyright © 2018 by Anh Do
Illustrations by Jeremy Ley

All rights reserved. Published by Scholastic Inc. *Publishers since 1920.* SCHOLASTIC and associated logos are trademarks and/or registered trademarks of Scholastic Inc.

The publisher does not have any control over and does not assume any responsibility for author or third-party websites or their content.

No part of this publication may be reproduced, stored in a retrieval system, or transmitted in any form or by any means, electronic, mechanical, photocopying, recording, or otherwise, without written permission of the publisher. For information regarding permission, write to Scholastic Inc., Attention: Permissions Department, 557 Broadway, New York, NY 10012.

This book is a work of fiction. Names, characters, places, and incidents are either the product of the author's imagination or are used fictitiously, and any resemblance to actual persons, living or dead, business establishments, events, or locales is entirely coincidental.

ISBN 978-1-338-30580-7

10 9 8 7 6 5 4   21 22 23 24

Printed in the United States of America   40
First U.S. printing 2020

Typeset in Bizzle-Chizzle, featuring Hola Bisou and Handblock.

ANH DO

illustrated by Jeremy Ley

NINJA KID 2

FLYING NINJA!

■SCHOLASTIC

ONE

My name is Nelson. Until recently, I was just a normal kid, maybe even a **nerdy** kid . . . and I was OK with that.

But on my tenth birthday, everything changed when I found out that I was the **last ninja on EARTH.**

So now . . . I'm the **NINJA KID!**

Only problem is, I'm not that good at it. I still feel more like a nerd than a ninja.

In fact, I could be the **world's NERDIEST ninja.**

Sometimes I accidentally wear my underpants back-to-front . . .

UNDieS BaCK-To-FRoNT

I'm scared of **spiders**...

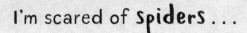

AHHH!

And I'm scared of **heights**.

Sometimes I daydream about being
the HANDSOMEST ninja . . .

Or the **COOLEST** ninja...

But I'm not that handsome or cool, so being a **nerdy** ninja kid will have to do for now.

And using my brain has actually been working for me so far. Like last week, when our town was overrun by **spiders** the size of **dump trucks.**

Being handsome or cool wouldn't have helped much . . .

HaNDSoMe NeLSoN

But being **clever** _was_ useful, because
I used my brain to come up with a way to
shrink all the spiders back to normal size.

And I also managed to **shrink** the bad guy to the size of a fly!

But the strangest thing was, he looked like a meaner, **skinnier** version of my dad!

BaD Guy

My DaD

So, this ninja thing is really exciting but also a bit **crazy** at the same time.

Luckily, I have Mom, Grandma Pat, and Cousin Kenny to help me get through it all!

The four of us live on a junkyard in the town of Duck Creek. Mom works as a cleaner, and my Grandma Pat runs the junkyard—but she's also an inventor.

It's really cool that Kenny lives with us, too, 'cause he's my best friend.

KeNNy

"Mom, Grandma," I said that morning when I sat down for breakfast, "you know that guy in the chopper? Well, just before he flew away, I saw his face, and he looked very familiar ... **Is he my dad?**"

"No!" said Mom.

"He's **not** your father," said Grandma. "But there is a reason he looks so much like your father ..."

Grandma paused. "He is your father's twin brother."

What the?!

"His name is Doctor Andrew Kane," Grandma continued.

"So . . . he's **my uncle?!**" I said. "Is he a ninja, too?"

"He is not," Grandma replied. "He and your father are identical twins. They were almost exactly the same . . . until they turned ten.

DaD

DaD'S
TWiN
BRoTHeR

"Then your father developed the skills of the ninja. But Andrew did not. This made him **very angry**. He felt like he was cheated."

"Was he cheated?" I asked.

"No, not at all. We all have different skills and abilities, and although Andrew was not given **strength** or *speed*, he was given **amazing intelligence**. He became my student, and I taught him everything I knew about science and the art of inventing.

"But Andrew was never happy with who he was, and he didn't see his great intelligence as a gift. He always felt as though he was less than his brother. So he **craved power.**"

"Then what happened, Grandma?"

"He stole all my research and ran away to make himself **more powerful**...

... and now he is back."

"Well, we've got nothing to worry about," Kenny piped up. "'Cause he's as **small** as a jelly bean!"

"No, Kenny, we have **a lot** to worry about," Grandma replied. "Andrew will easily invent a way to make himself big again—and then he will return, **angrier** than ever."

"But what does he want? Why does he keep hanging around Duck Creek?"

"He wants power. He wants control. He has allowed his anger to change him. And he thinks the way to **power** is through the purple stones."

RaRe PuRPLe SToNe

I remembered the rare stone I'd found in the forest. I couldn't believe I **threw it away** to scare a spider! We'd never find it again!

"But how does a stone give someone power, Grandma?" I asked.

"No one knows for sure, but people believe the stones give their bearers the power to control the thoughts of others," Grandma replied.

"That's why he's come back to Duck Creek after all this time," said Mom. "He thinks the stones are around here, and he wants to find them."

"How do we **STOP** him?" I asked.

"We need to be prepared," Grandma said. "Let's go, boys; we've got some training to do!"

TWO

Kenny and I followed Grandma out to her workshop hidden in our junkyard. That's right, our grandma has a **secret workshop** in the junkyard.

I reckon if you made a list of coolest grandmas, ours would be number one.

LIST OF COOLEST GRANDMAS:

#3

Grandmas who play heavy-metal guitar.

PReTTy CooL

#2

Grandmas who ride awesome motorcycles.

eVeN CooLeR

VROOOM!

#1 Grandmas with a secret ninja workshop.

THe CooleST!

When we entered the workshop, Grandma pressed a button and a secret cupboard opened up in the wall. **What the?!** It was full of super-awesome inventions we'd never seen before!

"I was going to save these for later," Grandma said, "but it seems the time has come."

Grandma reached into the cupboard and pulled out the **chunkiest** backpack I had ever seen.

"That's one fat backpack, Grandma!" said Cousin Kenny. "Please tell me it's full of doughnuts!"

"This backpack is **very** special," Grandma replied. She pushed a button on the backpack and **WHAM!** The bag transformed before our eyes!

Solar panels sprung out of the top, a handlebar came out of the side, and twin engines popped out of the back!

"Why would anyone want a backpack with a handlebar?" Kenny asked.

"Because it's not a backpack, Kenny. It's a **jetpack!**" said Grandma.

"A solar-powered jetpack!" I said. **"AWESOME!"**

"C'mon, boys, I'll show you how it works!"

"Can I go first?" asked Kenny.

"As long as you listen **very carefully** to my instructions and don't get distracted!" Grandma replied.

"Of course I won't get—hey, can anyone else smell barbecue?" Kenny was **sniffing** the air.

Grandma looked at Kenny.

"Just kidding, Grandma!" he said, smiling.

As Grandma strapped the jetpack across Kenny's shoulders, she adjusted a few buttons. "I'll just turn this down a bit so you can't go too high and hurt yourself," she said.

"See this throttle? Push it forward to take off and accelerate. Pull it back to slow down, and—"

"What does this **X button** do?" Kenny interrupted, pressing the X button.

Kenny screamed as he **lifted off** the ground and started **spinning** around.

AAAAAAGHHH!

"The **X button** is to **SPIN!**" Grandma yelled. "Pull back on the throttle to come back down, Kenny!"

"**OK!**" screamed Kenny.

Kenny accidentally did a **loop the loop** before landing on the ground.

WHOA! YIKES!

"You alright, Kenny?" I asked.

"Yeah, I think I've mastered it!" he said. "Why don't you have a go, Nelson?"

"I don't know . . ." I muttered.

I wasn't feeling good about this because I really **don't like heights**.

"Maybe Kenny can be the jetpack guy," I said to Grandma. "Anyone who can do spins like that is a natural!"

"No thanks!" said Kenny.

He pulled out a granola bar and started munching away.

"You boys are letting your fear take over," Grandma said. "Clear your mind, listen to my guidance, and give it a try."

If there was one thing I was good at, it was **giving things a try**.

I took a deep breath, then nodded.

Grandma strapped the jetpack onto my back.

"OK," said Grandma. "Rule number one: Don't touch anything until I've **FINISHED** my instructions!"

"Especially not the **X button!**" Kenny said with a mouthful of granola bar.

"Rule number two," Grandma continued. "To take off, slowly push the throttle forward."

I nodded, listening carefully.

"Rule number three," Grandma said. "To steer, hold on to the handlebar and lean the way you want to go."

She demonstrated by *leaning* her
body to the left, then to the right.

"Rule number four: To come down, pull
back on the throttle."

"I wish you'd told me all that," Kenny
said.

"You didn't give me a chance!" Grandma replied. "You're good to go, Nelson," she said, giving me the **thumbs-up.**

I was still feeling super nervous, but I wanted to give it a try. I did as Grandma said, took a deep breath, and cleared my mind.

I s-l-o-w-l-y pushed the throttle forward. It **fell right off** the handlebar!

CLUNK!

"Oops!" said Grandma. "Let me put a bit more tape on that."

"OK, try one more time," said Grandma.

"Focus, Nelson," I said to myself, and s-l-o-w-l-y pushed the throttle forward.

I lifted a few inches off the ground, then dropped back down.

"Push it a little farther," Grandma said.

"Can do!" I said. But I pushed it too far, and . . .

WHOoOoOSS

I ended up in a tree!

"Sorry!" I called down to Grandma.

"You both need a lot more practice," Grandma said. "But not now. It looks like it's about to rain, and if it's cloudy, the jetpack will run out of power."

Just then Mom appeared from our house.

It's time for the dentist!

I was concentrating so hard on the jetpack lesson that I totally forgot I had a **DENTIST** appointment before school!

NOOOOOOO!

"Can I please stay up here instead?!"

THREE

I hate everything about the dentist.
The **bright** lights . . .

The **scary-looking** scrapy tools . . .

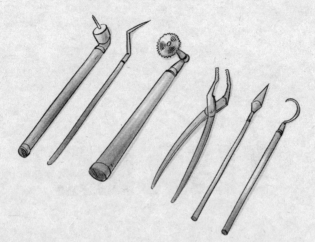

The way the dentist tries to talk to you while they've got their fingers in your mouth.

A lot of kids have **nightmares** about ghosts. My nightmares are about dentists! I'd rather fight another army of giant spiders than go to the dentist!

PiNG!

Do you know what would be **really** scary?

A GIANT
SPIDER
DENTIST!

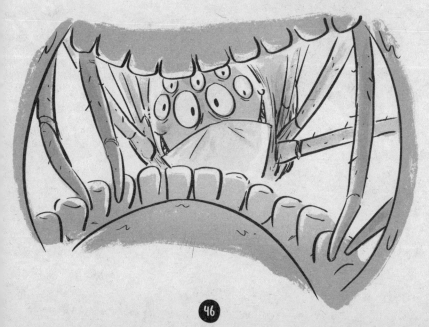

Imagine it using all its tools on you . . .

AT ONCE!

Even though we were already sitting in the waiting room, I tried one last time to get out of my appointment.

"Mom, I'm a ninja, I don't need to go to the dentist anymore."

"Ninjas need healthy teeth, too, Nelson!" Mom replied.

I whispered to Kenny, "I wish we had brought the jetpack so we could escape."

"Why would we want to escape?" Kenny asked. "Going to the dentist is **the best!**"

Kenny loved the dentist. He was so weird.

The dentist came out to the waiting room. She wasn't the dentist we usually had. She wasn't scary-looking at all!

She had a kind face and the **brightest** teeth I'd ever seen.

"Hi, Nelson and Kenny, I'm Doctor Dee Kay. Now, who wants to go fir-"

Before she'd even finished her sentence, Kenny had **raced** into her room, jumped onto the dentist's chair, and put the funny glasses on.

Mom stayed in the waiting room while Dr. Kay and I joined Kenny.

YEAH!

"I like your enthusiasm, Kenny!" Dr. Kay said as she pulled on gloves and a mask. "So, what have you boys been up to this morning?"

"We've been trying out a jetpack," Kenny said. "Because Nelson is a **nahhajaahhhhaaa!**"

It's lucky Dr. Kay put her fingers in Kenny's mouth when she did, because he was about to tell her I was a **NINJA!**

Kenny is hopeless with secrets. He gets **overexcited** and forgets they're called secrets for a reason!

Dr. Kay seemed really nice. But while she was checking Kenny's teeth, I started to get this strange feeling something bad was about to happen.

Thunder **rumbled** outside, and I could hear rain pattering on the roof. Then, suddenly, I saw something **seriously NUTS** . . .

WHAT THE?!

The dentist's drill had **jumped off** the bench and was doing **backflips** in the air!

"What is going on with that **crazy drill?!**" I shouted to Kenny and Dr. Kay.

But just as soon as it started, the drill dropped back to the bench. When they turned around, everything looked normal.

"What's so crazy about it?" Kenny asked.

"It was doing flips and dancing in the air!" I exclaimed.

Kenny and Dr. Kay looked at me like I was completely bonkers!

"I've heard all sorts of **excuses** to get out of a dentist's appointment," Dr. Kay said. "But a dancing drill? Ha! That's the best!" She looked at Kenny. "You're all done, Kenny. Your turn, Nelson."

I couldn't believe Kenny and Dr. Kay hadn't seen the dancing drill!

Was I losing my mind?

I moved slowly over to the dentist's chair and put the funny glasses on.

"Open wide," Dr. Kay said.

I opened my mouth.

More thunder **clapped** outside. Then, as I stared at the bright lights, they started **flickering**.

Dr. Kay looked up, too. "Just a little power surge." She shrugged.

I had a feeling it was more serious than that, but for the rest of my checkup nothing else strange happened.

Dr. Kay made lots of sounds while she looked at my teeth and gums.

Aha . . .

Hmmm . . .

Excellent!

If my teeth were a movie, I reckon she would've given it **five stars!**

"All done, Nelson," Dr. Kay said.

I couldn't believe my appointment had gone so quickly, and it hadn't hurt at all!

"Because you boys have been so good at looking after your teeth, I have a reward for you," Dr. Kay said. "Wait here."

Dr. Kay left the room. Kenny and I looked at each other excitedly.

"Maybe she's getting us a lollipop!" Kenny said.

The rain on the roof got louder. Then **ALL** the tools in the room started

GOING NUTS!

FLiCK!

CLUNK!

ZiNG!

Drills, irrigators, and electric toothbrushes all came to life! The chair was going **up** and **down** by itself!

CLUNK!

CLUNK!

Lightning crashed outside, and then the tools came **straight for us!**

DRRRRRRR!

I used my ninja skills to fend them away. I kicked at a few **angry** drills while Kenny used a hand mirror as a shield.

But there were way too many of them. The suction machine was about to go up Kenny's nose!

EEEEEK!

Then the rain **died down**, and suddenly everything went back to normal.

WHAT WAS GOING ON?!

"That was close!" said Kenny. "I did **not** come to the dentist to get a nose job!"

I had this **crazy idea** that the rain was somehow affecting all the electronic equipment. *Could it be?* Surely not.

Dr. Kay came back in. "There's been a lot of noise in here. What have you boys been up to?" she asked.

Kenny was about to explain, but
I covered his mouth. "Nothing! Just
getting excited about our reward!"

"Glad to hear it," Dr. Kay said. "Now
close your eyes and hold out your hands."
I loved this game . . .

Hmmm, it definitely didn't feel like a lollipop . . .

I opened my eyes.

Dr. Kay had given us each a box of **dental floss!** I was a little disappointed, but Kenny was p^ump^ed.

"Thanks, Dr. Kay! Best reward EVER!"

WOW!

As Mom drove us to school, Kenny and I looked at each other. Did we really just get attacked by dental tools, or was it some **weird dream?**

The rain was still falling, and I thought I could see a helicopter flying in the distance. Was it Dr. Kane's chopper? I didn't know for sure . . .

Could this morning get any weirder?!

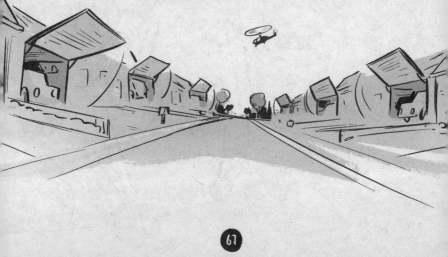

Then, as we were driving, I noticed all the traffic lights were **flashing**. And I saw everyone's garage doors **flapping up and down** like crazy.

HUH?!

YAY!

There was definitely something
strange going on in Duck Creek today,
and I couldn't help thinking that Dr. Kane
was probably behind it.

FOUR

By the time Mom dropped us at school, it was **pouring** rain!

The rain was getting heavier, so I sprinted toward our classroom. But Kenny just kept walking as if it were a normal, sunny day!

"What are you doing?" I yelled out to him.

"I read somewhere that you get **LESS** wet if you **walk** through a storm," Kenny said. He was drenched.

"And how's that working out for you?"
I asked.

"Not so good! RUN!"

Kenny and I sprinted through the rain.
Huge puddles were forming all around us.

Before I became a ninja, I would've tripped in them for sure. But now I was able to **dodge** them easily.

Poor Kenny couldn't see the puddles until it was too late! He stepped in a huge puddle, **splashing** water everywhere and soaking both of us!

By the time Kenny and I arrived outside class, we were **totally saturated.**

I heard some strange noises coming from inside the classroom.

"Did you hear that?" I asked Kenny.

Kenny pushed open the door, and there
was Mr. Fletcher, standing on his desk
screaming. A vacuum cleaner had come to
life and was attacking the class!

What was going on?

The machine was chasing the kids
around the room, making an awful
sucking sound.

SLURP!

"I'll go and get help!" Mr. Fletcher
squealed before jumping off the desk
and running out the door.

Charles Brock, the class bully, followed closely behind. "Outta my way, you bunch of lowlifes!"

But the vacuum cleaner blocked his path, so he turned and pushed his way back into the crowd. "Let me back in, you losers!"

Charles Brock wasn't the only kid completely freaking out. Kenny was frozen with fear, too!

He hated vacuum cleaners as much as I hated going to the dentist. **THIS** was Kenny's worst nightmare.

"I hate vacuum cleaners!" said Kenny.

"They suck!"

It was hard to argue with him!

"If we unplug the vacuum from the electrical outlet, that might shut it down," I said to Kenny.

There was just one problem with this plan.

The vacuum cleaner was now **in front** of the outlet, blocking our way.

SLURP!

"You go left, I'll go right," I said to Kenny.

Kenny shook his head.

"OK, you go right, I'll go left!" I suggested.

Kenny shook his head again!

I realized Kenny was **too scared** to move at all.

"No worries, Kenny—**plan B.** I'll shut the thing off, you be my lookout!"

Kenny nodded and gave me a thumbs-up.

A huge bolt of lightning struck outside, which seemed to make the vacuum even angrier! It reared toward the ceiling and then started chasing Sarah around the classroom.

VRRREEEEE!

Sarah is one of the quickest kids in our class, but the vacuum was even quicker. It pounced on Sarah and **wrapped** itself around her like a python.

HELP!

I liked Sarah. A lot. She's one of the nicest girls at school. I really didn't want to watch her get **squeezed** by a vacuum cleaner. But this vacuum cleaner seemed so powerful! How was I supposed to stop it?!

Be brave, I told myself. So I did a **ninja roll** underneath the desks and got behind the vacuum.

"**Rock and roll, Nelson!**" Kenny shouted.

Luckily, the vacuum cleaner hadn't noticed me. Sarah hadn't seen me either.

I tried to pull the vacuum off Sarah, but it was seriously heavy. I couldn't budge it! The vacuum was **squeezing** Sarah tighter.

I had to find another way to free her **and fast!**

I couldn't reach the electrical outlet, but I thought if I could block the end of the vacuum, it might lose some of its power.

I looked around for something that could do the job... BINGO!

CHALKBOARD ERASER

"Kenny! Throw me the eraser!"

Kenny's throw was way off, **bouncing** off the ceiling fan, onto the wall, and then rebounding.

PiNG!

I s-t-r-e-t-c-h-e-d out my foot and flicked it up to catch the eraser. My ninja instincts were kicking in! Now I had to try to block up the vacuum. Only problem was, it was waving all over the place like a **crazy, giant** garden hose!

I rolled closer to the vacuum cleaner.
Just as it **whipped** past me, I threw the
eraser.

FLING!

Got it! The eraser jammed into the
end of the vacuum. The awful sucking
sound changed to a high-pitched whine.
The hose loosened its grip, and Sarah
burst free.

Suddenly, the vacuum went limp and stopped altogether. The room was quiet.

Everyone looked over. **Charles Brock** was standing next to the electrical outlet with the plug in his hand.

"You saved me, Charles! Thank you!" Sarah said.

WHAT THE?!

Sarah thought *Charles* was the reason the vacuum had let her go?

"Anytime," Charles said. He was always taking credit for things he didn't do.

"What about Nelson?" cried Kenny.

"Nelson? **Nelson's useless!** Look at him! First sign of danger, he hides under the table!" said Charles.

Truth was, I didn't look like **a hero** at all. I looked like a fool sprawled out on the floor.

Sarah probably thought I was a big coward. Maybe one day she'll learn the truth. But for now, I'd just have to let it go.

Just then, Mr. Fletcher returned to the classroom. He looked around nervously. "Er, um . . . yes, looks like I've got the situation under control. Back in your seats, everyone!"

Today was getting **stranger** by the second!

FiVE

When we got home after school, Mom and Grandma said they'd had really weird days, too! While Mom was at work, cleaning the local gym, the exercise bikes and treadmills went **nuts,** and all the people on them were **thrown** across the room!

Grandma's day was **even crazier!**

Her Zap-O-Matic came to life, escaped the workshop, and started **shrinking** everything in its path: trees, cars, even a few unlucky animals!

OOPS!

Luckily, Grandma zapped them back to their normal size after the storm had passed.

ZAP!

"Why is everything attacking us?" I asked.

"We think someone has infected everything electric with a virus," Mom said.

"Like the flu?" Kenny asked. "I thought I saw that vacuum cleaner sneezing."

"It's sort of like the flu," Grandma replied. "I have been studying this closely for a while now. The virus rests inside machines until it rains, and then it makes them **come to life.**"

"So that's why the dentist's drill was going nuts!" I said.

WELCOME
TO
DUCK CREEK

"It's getting **worse** with each storm," Mom said. "If it continues, it won't be safe to stay in Duck Creek."

"Who would want machines taking over Duck Creek?" Kenny asked.

I had some idea—the same person who created **giant spiders!** "Dr. Kane!"

Grandma nodded.

"But *why* is he doing all this?" I asked.

"I think he's trying to get rid of all the people in the town so he can look for the purple stones," said Grandma.

"But a machine virus? There must be an easier way to get everyone out of town!" I said.

"Sure there is!" Kenny chimed in. "Two-for-one cheeseburgers at Harry's Burgers across the river! That would clear this town in minutes!"

"So, anyway, how can we cure this machine virus?" I asked.

"I'm working on a code that will shut down the virus," Grandma said.

"But there are **thousands** of electronic devices in this town!" I said. "How will you fix them all?"

"I've developed a way to shrink the code and turn it into **e-dust** so it can be sprinkled into the clouds. Then, when it rains, the code will spread all over Duck Creek."

"How will you get the code into the clouds, Grandma?" I asked.

"I won't," Grandma said. Then she pointed to me. **"You will!"**

"What?!" I almost fell off my chair.

"That's why Grandma has been teaching you to use the jetpack," Mom added.

"But won't the jetpack take on a life of its own next time it rains?" Kenny asked. "It'll be **twisting** and **turning** more than an ice-skater with an **itchy** butt!"

"Solar-powered machines *aren't* affected by the virus," Grandma said.

"But I'm hopeless at the jetpack—I couldn't get past a tree! I'll never get up into **the clouds!**" I said.

"That's why we're heading out now for more practice!" Grandma said.

Kenny pointed at me. "Ground Control salutes you, Captain Nelson!"

As we walked outside, I very much doubted whether I could actually do this.

"Nelson, I really need you **to focus** this time," Grandma said. She was already attaching the jetpack to my back.

"Want a grape to calm your nerves?"
Kenny asked, holding out a bunch.

"No thanks, Kenny," I said.

"Food always makes me feel better!"
Kenny said.

That was true. Whether Kenny was
happy, sad, angry, or nervous, food
ALWAYS made him feel better.

Unless it was carrots. Kenny hated
carrots!

Blurgh!

"Nelson, we don't have much time,"
Grandma said. "Push the throttle
forward."

"Not too soft, not too hard, just
right!" Kenny said.

I didn't want to end up in a tree again.
I didn't want to let Grandma down either.

I calmed my nerves, then pushed the
throttle . . .

This time I didn't fly into the trees.
I hovered at a safe height.

"Nice work, Nelson!" Grandma yelled.

As I got more confident with the
jetpack, I **soared higher** into the sky.

At first I was a little shaky, but the
longer I spent in the air, the more in
control I felt. Soon, I was soaring through
the sky like an eagle!

It was such a COOL feeling!

I glanced down at Kenny and Grandma
on the ground. They looked like ants!
Well, ants with two arms that were
wearing clothes and throwing grapes...
WHAAAAAT?!
A grape hit me right on the forehead!

PING!

HEY!

Grandma was **throwing** Kenny's grapes at me!

"What are you doing, Grandma?" I yelled down to her.

"Teaching you how to **dodge** and **weave!**" she said. Grandma threw another grape, and it hit me in the neck! "Lean in the direction you want to go!" Grandma yelled, hurling another grape.

Then another.

"Hey!" Kenny said. "Don't waste them!"

But there was no stopping Grandma.
Her throws were so quick and accurate!
Maybe she used to be a baseball pitcher!

Almost every grape that Grandma
threw hit me. But then, little by little, I
got better at weaving. Soon, Grandma
couldn't hit me no matter how hard she
tried!

WHOOSH!

None of the grapes ended up on the ground though, because Kenny was **running** around under me catching them all in his mouth!

"This ninja is *grape* at dodging! Get it?" Kenny yelled out through a mouthful of grapes.

"**Watch out!**" Grandma called to me.

I looked up and saw that I was just about to fly **into a phone tower!**

AHHH!

I leaned hard to the right
and just missed the tower. PHEW!

Suddenly, a light started flashing
on the jetpack.

"I think that's enough practice for
now!" Grandma called out. "When you see
that light, it means the jetpack is nearly
out of power and you have to come down
immediately."

"OK!" I shouted. I couldn't wait to take the jetpack off after my near miss.

"Welcome back to Earth, **Flying Ninja!**" Kenny beamed.

"You've improved," Grandma said. "But you need to maintain concentration."

"OK, Grandma," I replied.

"Soon you'll be able to **dodge** an entire fruit salad! Now follow me; I've got something else to show you."

When we got back to the workshop,
Grandma wheeled out the bike she had
invented for me. It's almost exactly like a
normal bike . . . except it runs on bananas.

"No offense, Grandma, but we've seen
that bike before," Kenny said.

"You have," Grandma agreed. "But not with a **turbo-powered engine!**" She **revved** the banana bike, and it roared like a lion!

"**WHOA!**" Kenny and I said together. "And it only needs a few extra bananas to run!" Grandma grinned.

"I've got something for you, too, Kenny," Grandma said, hurrying back into the workshop.

When she came out again, she was holding Kenny's skateboard. It now had a motor attached, too!

"What have you done to my awesome skateboard?" Kenny asked.

"I've made it even **MORE awesome**," Grandma said, "with a **carrot-powered motor!**"

"But I hate carrots!"

"Exactly!" Grandma laughed. "So there's no chance of you eating all the fuel!"

Even Kenny couldn't help laughing at that.

Kenny tried out his carrot-powered skateboard. It was **lightning quick,** and when Kenny got air, he got serious AIR!

WOO!

YEAH!

"I love it, Grandma!" Kenny shouted.

"Glad to hear it," Grandma replied. "But that's enough training for today. You boys need to rest before your zoo excursion in the morning."

"Zoohoo!" Kenny yelled.

"Only one more sleep!" I said.

"I'm going to bed **NOW**," Kenny said.

"So tomorrow comes quicker!"

GOOD NIGHT!

SiX

Kenny and I both woke up super early the next morning.

"I love the zoo so much I could live there!" Kenny said as he helped himself to breakfast.

"Good news," Grandma said, joining us at the table. "There's no rain forecast for today."

"Looks like it's going to be fine with **NO chance of crazy machines.** My favorite kind of day!" I said.

We definitely didn't want Dr. Kane ruining our zoo excursion with his e-virus!

"Take the jetpack just in case," Grandma said.

"Do I have to?" I asked. "It's soooo much heavier than my normal backpack!" But the real reason I didn't want to take the jetpack was . . .

I didn't want the **responsibility.**

Grandma had this strange ability to always sense my fear.

"Believe in yourself, Nelson," she said. "Your instincts are strong."

I nodded, seriously hoping she was right.

"One more thing," Grandma added. "I've finished the e-code."

"Cool!" said Kenny. "So what now?"

"I've crushed it into thousands of tiny molecules and put the e-dust in a tin inside Nelson's jetpack for when the time comes. I've packed a few other things for you, too," Grandma said.

"Want a lift, boys?" Mom asked. "You don't want to miss the zoo bus."

"No chance of that—now my banana bike is **turbo-powered!**" I said.

"And my skateboard is carrot-charged!" Kenny said. "Wish it was cereal-charged instead."

He shoveled a huge spoonful of cornflakes into his mouth.

Cruising to school on our supercharged wheels was the **best!**

We were making great time. It even looked like we'd get to school early . . . for the first time ever!

Kenny pulled out a granola bar and started eating it.

"Yuck! It's carrot-flavored!" cried Kenny. **"I hate carrots!"**

Then his eyes widened as he came up with an idea. "Nelson . . . I wonder if this carrot-flavored granola bar will make my skateboard go **even faster?!"**

"I think that's a bad idea, Kenny!" I called out.

But it was too late. Kenny had already stuck the granola bar into the skateboard's engine. **Uh-oh.**

There was a puff of black smoke and then a **GURGLE** . . .

GURGLE . . .

GURGLE . . .

Kenny's skateboard **slooooowed** to a stop.

"Oops!" said Kenny.

"I told you it was a bad idea!" I said.

"Well . . . can't you just use some of your **awesome new skills** to fix it?"

"I'm a ninja, Kenny, not a mechanic!"

We both sat on the footpath and picked all the granola-bar bits out of the engine. It took us ages, but eventually we got Kenny's skateboard going again. Problem was, by the time we got to school, the zoo bus had left!

Zoo Bus

"I'm really sorry," Kenny mumbled.

"It's OK," I said, planning our next move. "I think we've got enough bananas and carrots to make it to the zoo. **Let's go!**"

SEVEN

Kenny and I got to the zoo just as our class was heading through the gates. "Perfect timing!" I said to Kenny.

The first animals our class visited were the zebras. I was watching the mother zebra feeding her baby when Sarah walked over.

"Did you know that every zebra has a unique stripe pattern?" she said.

I couldn't believe Sarah was talking to me. The most she had ever said to me before today was "Hi!"

"I didn't know that," I replied. "Did you know that zebras can sleep standing up?"

"Wow, can they really?" Sarah replied. We both loved zebras! This was **great!**

We walked to the Rainforest Aviary next. It was **AWESOME.** There were so many stunning birds it was hard to know where to look first!

"It's so beautiful in here," Sarah said. "It feels just like a real rainforest."

"They've even got fake rain!" Kenny said, amazed.

He was right; raindrops were falling. But they weren't coming from within the aviary—they were **falling** from **the clouds!**

"Er, that's real rain, Kenny!" Sarah said.

Uh-oh! That meant Dr. Kane's e-virus could be activated! And Mom said it was getting worse every time it rained!

Suddenly, a family of meerkats ran right past us.

That's weird . . .

I must have imagined it . . .

But then the meerkats were followed
by a sun bear . . .

and a rhino!

"Aww, it's nice that they let the animals
out to play," Kenny said.

"They're not supposed to be out!"
Sarah said worriedly.

"Their cage doors are electronic," I realized. "The rain has made them open!"

"Uh-oh!" Kenny said.

"Double uh-oh," I added. "Look!"

The e-virus had infected the animal waste truck, too! It was driving by itself and **hurling poo** everywhere.

FLING!

"Duck!" I yelled.

"Where's the duck?" Kenny looked around.

"No! Duck your head!"

Sarah, Kenny, and I ducked just in time to avoid a huge spray of poo.

Mr. Fletcher wasn't so lucky . . .

SPLAT!

The rain continued to fall, and more and more cages were opening. There were animals running around

EVERYWHERE!

ELEPHANTS, GIRAFFES, TURTLES, PENGUINS, TIGERS, MONKEYS, LEMURS!

People were screaming as the animals roamed around like they were in the jungle.

"Sorry, Sarah," I said. "Kenny and I have to . . . um . . . get out of here."

"Where are you going?" she asked.

"We just have to . . ." I mumbled.

"They're running away 'cause they're **chickens!**" shouted Charles, who was crouched behind a group of kids.

Oh man! Sarah already thought I was a coward from what had happened with the vacuum cleaner, and now it was going to look like I was fleeing from danger **again!** But we had no choice.

I watched as a bunch of huge gorillas escaped from their cages. "Sorry, Sarah!" I grabbed Kenny and off we ran.

Sarah looked really disappointed in me as we hurried away from the class.

"Scaredy-cats!" Charles yelled.

As Kenny and I ran, I looked inside the backpack. At first, all I could see was the tin containing the e-dust.

Then I unzipped a hidden compartment.
Grandma had packed our **superhero**
outfits!

They weren't the fanciest of disguises—
mine was a sock and Kenny's was just a
glove—but Grandma had needed to come
up with something fast. (And she's an
inventor after all, not a fashion designer.)

We quickly hid behind a tree and put
them on.

I hopped onto my banana bike, and
Kenny jumped on his carrot skateboard.
As Kenny and I raced back toward
our class, we heard a boy yelling, "Help!
I want my mommy!"

It was Charles. The gorillas were using him as a human football!

"We have to save him," I said to Kenny.

"Do we? *Really?!*" Kenny asked.

"Yes! Hey, gorillas!" I called out. "You like bananas?!"

VROOOM!

The gorillas sniffed the air. They dropped Charles . . . **and bounded after me!**

I revved the banana bike again and set off through the zoo with the gorillas in hot pursuit.

I jumped over the leopard seal pool . . .

. . . skidded past the panda pen, and screeched into the gorilla enclosure.

SCREEEEEECH!

Once the gorillas were all inside, I closed the gate and sped back to Kenny.

He was leading the giraffes back to their enclosure with the smell from his carrot skateboard!

Sarah and the rest of the class cheered us on, not realizing it was Kenny and me!

Sarah called out, **"Hey!** You can leave the zebras to me!"

She found a bucket of dried grass,
and all the zebras immediately started to
follow her back to their enclosure.

I had to hand it to Sarah; she knew a lot about zebras!

After we'd led the rhinos, elephants, and turtles back into their enclosures, Kenny and I shared a massive sigh of relief. Finally, all the animals were back inside. Better still, it had stopped raining, and the sun was coming out.

"That was **epic!**" Kenny said. "I love the zoo!"

It seemed like everything was back to normal . . . until we heard a familiar noise.

WHUP-WHUP-WHUP-WHUP!

It was the red helicopter. *Dr. Kane's* red helicopter!

"You're wasting your time!" Dr. Kane shouted down at us through his megaphone. "Next time it rains,

Duck Creek will be MINE!"

"You know," said Kenny, "if that guy's a doctor, I'd like a second opinion!"

"We have to get the e-dust into the clouds—**now!**" I said to Kenny.

"*We?!*" Kenny exclaimed.

"I can't control the jetpack!"

"Neither can I!" I said. "I almost flew into the phone tower!"

"Remember what Grandma said: Believe in yourself, Nelson," Kenny said.

I'd never heard him sound so wise!

I closed my eyes and imagined flying high and dodging everything in my path.

"I can do this," I said to myself, preparing for the flight of my life.

I took a deep breath, then pushed the button on my backpack, transforming it into the **SOLAR-POWERED JETPACK.**

"Wish me luck," I said to Kenny.

"Good luck, Ninja Kid!" he said,
taking a banana out of his bag, about
to eat it. Then he changed his mind.
"Actually, you take this." He put the
banana in my backpack. "Oh, and this . . ."
He put an apple into my backpack. "You
might get hungry up there!"

"And remember, Nelson, the **X button** makes you spin like **CRAZY!**"

"Thanks, Kenny. You're the **best sidekick** ever. Here I go!"

I pushed the throttle forward and **soared** into the sky.

EiGHT

Dr. Kane wasn't happy about me joining him in the air.

"You've made a **BIG** mistake!" he called out. Then he added, "Why don't you just leave town and let me do my important work?!"

"**Yeah right,**" I said. "You want us all to leave so that you can get your hands on the purple stones!"

"What?! How did you know?" It seemed like that last line shocked him. "Who are you, boy? And how do you know my **PLANS?!**"

He flew his helicopter straight toward me. I weaved out of the way just in time. It was lucky I'd had all that practice dodging Grandma's grapes!

As I looked down, I realized the whole class was staring at me from the ground. **"Watch out!"** Kenny shouted.

I looked back up. Dr. Kane had dropped a **HUGE net** from his helicopter!

I didn't have time to weave around it. There was **NOTHING** I could do! The net struck me hard and sent me **hurtling** toward the ground.

UH-OH!

As the world spun around, my thoughts did, too. I thought about my mom and grandma, my dad and Kenny. I remembered Kenny's crazy attempt at using the jetpack.

The **X** BUTTON!

I'd never used the SPIN function before, but I had no choice. I pressed it hard!

I went **SPINNING** through the air. I was moving so fast I couldn't see where I was going! **SPIN, SPIN, SPIN,** faster than I'd ever traveled in my life. I was flying out of control, but I managed to **shake** off the net!

WHOOOAAAA!

Everyone cheered from below!

Dr. Kane leaned out of the chopper, and he was super **ANGRY!** Now I got a really good look at him. He looked so much like my dad!

"Enough games!" he yelled, flying straight for me.

But **I dodged** him just in time!

The sun disappeared behind the clouds. I knew I could run out of solar power any second.

I had to stop Dr. Kane, but how?

As the helicopter **swerved** closer, I noticed an exhaust pipe sticking out of the back.

It reminded me of something . . . how we had shut down the vacuum cleaner!

I reached into the jetpack and pulled out . . .

Kenny's banana!

I knew it was crazy, but if I could throw a banana into the exhaust pipe, I might be able to stop Dr. Kane's helicopter.

"C'mon, Nelson," I said to myself. "You have to believe . . ."

I stared hard at the exhaust pipe and threw the banana with all my might . . .

FLiNG!

But it didn't even get close!

The blades of the helicopter **sprayed** bits of banana everywhere!

"Is that the best you can do? Attack me with fruit?" laughed Dr. Kane as he turned the helicopter around to come at me again.

I reached into my bag and felt around. All I had left was the apple!

Oh well, this will have to do . . .

"They say an apple a day keeps the doctor away!" I shouted back.

I focused my mind and threw the apple at the exhaust pipe as hard as I could.

It **hurtled** through the air like it was in s-l-o-w m-o-t-i-o-n . . .

And stuck!

CLUNK!

The helicopter blades suddenly slowed down, and the chopper **dipped.**

Dr. Kane was furious. "You'll regret this!" he shouted.

I'll be back!

The group below cheered as Dr. Kane turned and **spluttered** away into the distance.

But my mission wasn't over yet. I had to sprinkle Grandma's e-dust into the clouds. The sun was almost hidden now, and I could feel my jetpack running out of energy. I still needed to get higher.

I pressed the **X button** and went spiraling into the clouds. But just as I was about to start sprinkling the e-dust, I felt a drop of water hit my nose. It was starting to rain, and all the animal cages were beginning to open again. I had to act fast before the animals escaped.

But then the light started **flashing** on the jetpack.

Gulp!

Oh no, it was running out of power!
I was almost out of time!
I zoomed around the clouds and
sprinkled the e-dust as far and wide as
I could.

My jetpack was getting really **s-l-o-w,**
so I glided down toward the ground. But I
wasn't quick enough. With a final splutter,
my jetpack ran out of power!

AAAA

As I
tumbled
down
toward the ground,
I saw something awesome . . .

Sarah, Kenny, and some other kids from my class were holding out Dr. Kane's net to catch me.

I dropped safely onto the net, and the whole class **CHEERED** again!

The rain was falling heavily now, and as it bucketed down, it also **sprinkled** the e-dust everywhere.

It was like magic—all the cages locked back up, and the animal waste truck stopped flinging poo!

Sarah unrolled me from the net. "That was **AMAZING.** Who are you?"

"I'm Nel . . . I mean, the **NiNJA KiD,**" I stammered.

"And people call me **H-DUDE,**" Kenny said, popping up beside me.

"What does the H stand for?" Sarah asked him. "Hero?"

Hungry!

Sarah looked confused.

"I mean **handsome!**" Kenny changed his mind.

"My name's Sarah. Next time, I'd love to help you."

"That'd be great!" I said. "But right now, we gotta run!"

"Yeah, being handsome is a full-time job!" Kenny added.

"See you next time, Ninja Kid and H-Dude!" Sarah said.

"Bye, Sarah!" We hurried off.

When Kenny and I came back without our disguises, Sarah rushed over to us again.

"You just missed Ninja Kid and H-Dude!" she said excitedly. "They returned all the animals to their enclosures and scared off the man in the helicopter. Where have you been?"

"Ah . . ." I stuttered.

"They were hiding because they're **scaredy-cat losers!**" Charles said.

Kenny got angry again. "Scaredy-cat?!
We were the ones who saved—"

I put my hand over Kenny's mouth.
He was really struggling to keep our
identities a secret!

"What did you save?" Sarah asked.

"We saved . . . our best dance moves to
show you guys!" I said.

Then Kenny and I busted out our **best
routine.**

The whole class started laughing.

A part of me really wanted to tell them our secret, but I couldn't. I just let it go.

Then Mr. Fletcher reappeared from where he'd been hiding.

"Er, alright, well . . . I've got the situation under control . . . everyone hop on the bus," he said.

NiNE

At home, we told Mom and Grandma about everything that had happened at the zoo. Then we celebrated our victory over Dr. Kane by eating a banana-and-carrot cake!

We were so hungry after our crazy day that even though Kenny didn't like carrots, he was already on his third piece!

"I'm so relieved all the electronic devices have stopped attacking us!" Kenny said.

"Are you sure about that?" Mom asked and pointed above our heads.

AAHHHHHH!

An electric egg beater was coming straight for us!

"Don't panic!" Grandma said, pulling a remote control from behind her back. "It's just my **latest invention.**" Grandma steered the egg beater onto the ground.

"A remote-control egg beater?" I asked.

"You bet!" Grandma said. "Now I can bake a cake from another room!"

Even though all the electrical devices had returned to normal and we'd scared Dr. Kane away, I still couldn't relax. Seeing Dr. Kane up close had been so strange—like seeing my dad again.

"Do you think Dr. Kane knows something about Dad going missing?" I asked.

Mom looked to Grandma.

"Yes," Grandma said. "But that's a story for another day."

Nooooo!

I hate the waiting game!

"Today it's time to celebrate another successful mission!" said Mom.

Grandma smiled. "Well done, Kenny, and Nelson—the **FLYING NINJA!**"

I smiled, too.

Maybe . . . *just maybe* . . . I was starting to get the hang of being the Ninja Kid.

READ THEM ALL!

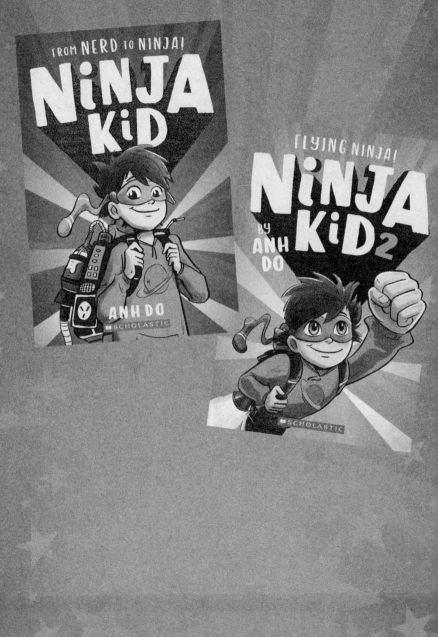